I078435b

THE GODS OF MOAB

THE GODS OF MOAB

By Stephen Mark Rainey

DAMNED RODAN PUBLISHING

2024

Damned Rodan Publishing
1023 Indian Trail
Martinsville, VA 24112
www.stephenmarkrainey.com

First Edition Printing

ISBN-13: 979-8-218-45931-4

For Kimberly, with all my love.

Chapter One:
9:24 PM

The headlights revealed only a glittering tunnel of ice and snow sloping down into a black, yawning pit that swallowed the road, the sagging tree limbs, even the light of the high beams. Warren glanced at the glowing GPS display on his phone, which revealed a hairpin turn ahead, a coiled viper poised to react violently if disturbed. Beyond it lay several more snaking curves, each certain to be as treacherous as this one. He was holding the Pathfinder to little more than a crawl, its four-wheel drive hardly a match for the deadly slick sheets of ice that covered the asphalt.

In the backseat, Kristin turned to peer out the rear glass. "I don't see anything," she said, her voice quavering. "Maybe it's nothing."

Her husband, Roger, also looked back, first giving Kristin a scowl. "Yeah, nothing. That's what it sounded like."

"What do you think it was?"

"Trees falling. Winter thunder. I don't know."

None of them spoke as Warren eased the vehicle down the slope that led to the hairpin. Halfway down, the electronic traction control light flared to life, and he felt the tires struggling for purchase on the slippery, uneven surface. So far, the Pathfinder was holding the road admirably, but the effort of keeping the heavy SUV from sliding out of control was taking its toll on his muscles and nerves. The GPS at least gave him an idea of what lay ahead. He just didn't like what he saw.

And there *was* something out there in the darkness. Something that made big, thunderous, crashing sounds. *Dangerous* sounds. They'd first heard the noises about two miles back, at first only vague and distant, barely discernible above the engine's rumbling, but now they were distinctly closer and more ominous.

"Trees falling," Anne said, glancing at him from the front passenger seat, aware of the direction his thoughts had taken. "It's the ice on the trees. It's too heavy."

The road had started out straight and relatively clear, and the GPS map had shown no sign of the long series of snaking curves they now faced. Clearly, *something* wasn't right, for they had somehow turned onto this unknown road without realizing it. Now his display would not even zoom out far enough to show their actual location. In any event, the road was too steep and narrow to turn around and go back they way they had come, even with the four-wheel drive. All they could do was press onward.

"Jesus, we're up high," Kristin said, peering out her window. Risking a glance into the darkness to his right, Warren saw numerous pinpoints of light far below. A few trees lined the road, but beyond them, it must be a sheer precipice. His fingers tightened on the steering wheel, and he forced himself to gaze straight ahead at the upcoming hairpin. The curve veered to the right, so if the vehicle began to slide, at least its momentum would carry it away from the drop-off.

Then they were on the curve. Warren sent the Pathfinder into the steep, 180-degree turn at no more than five miles per hour—but even so, the back end lurched and slid with stomach-wrenching suddenness, and he felt a sharp twinge of fear until the tires once again gripped a patch of exposed pavement with some assurance. As the road straightened out again, he realized that Anne's nails were digging into his right thigh.

"Damn it, woman," he said with forced levity. "If we go over the edge, that's only going to make it hurt worse."

Anne's relief was palpable, though certainly temporary. "If we die, I'm going to kill you for getting us lost," she said.

"Noted," he said, looking back at the map. Maybe a quarter mile to the next curve. Here, the grade wasn't quite as steep, but the ice was unbroken, the snow piled higher on either side of the road. Still, he allowed himself to relax a little before they reached the next harrowing passage.

"How much farther can this go on?" Kristin asked.

"I don't know."

She groaned, but Roger leaned back in his seat and closed his eyes. "Wake me when we get home."

"I'm glad you're so relaxed."

"So am I."

"Here we go again," Warren said, nodding toward the upcoming S-curve, which arced to the left. *Good God, if they started sliding here, they would go right over the edge.* "At least there's more snow than ice here," he said, with obligatory confidence. "It'll hold."

He felt it before he heard it: another vibration, faint at first, then deepening, becoming a heavy *boom-crash-boom* somewhere behind them, again closer and louder than before. It *had* to be trees falling. But when they came, the sounds were rhythmic, like some vast percussion from the heavens. Anne and Kristin looked back, and even Roger opened his eyes for a moment.

"What *is* that?" Kristin asked in bewildered frustration,

her sapphire eyes wide and bright in the darkness.

The question might have gnawed at him if he were not so intent on keeping the Pathfinder on the road, which was even more challenging now because he had built up some speed on the level stretch. A pair of low-hanging, claw-like branches appeared directly ahead, and they scraped noisily over the windshield, leaving a residue of white frost as the SUV pushed its way through them. Again, the back end swerved abruptly—to the right—forcing Warren to steer into the slide, and he saw the edge of the road rushing toward them. At the last second, the tires bit into crusty snow, and he managed to coax the Pathfinder back to the center of the road. He heard Anne and Kristin exhale sharply. Roger's eyes remained closed, his face impassive.

"There's no way to go back, is there?" Kristin asked, her voice plaintive, though she already knew the answer.

Warren just shook his head. The next curve, back to the right again, was already in view, not as sharp but steeper than the one they'd just negotiated.

He was just starting into the curve when the loud crash came, directly behind the car. Another and another—now from *above* them—and a heavy clump of snow splashed over the windshield. Anne drew back with an involuntary gasp. Then, with a deafening *crack-boom*, something heavy—a tree limb— hit the roof, causing the whole vehicle to shudder. Suddenly, the view ahead became pure movement, a whirling chiaroscuro of black, white, and gray, and he had a vague impression of long, finger-like limbs violently striking the glass. The steering wheel wrenched itself from his grip, and a chorus of shocked cries rose above the pounding and clattering. He tugged hard on the wheel, trying to regain control, but the front of the vehicle dipped violently, pitching him forward until the shoulder strap locked, seizing him like a wrestler's arm. Then they were sliding sideways, and he felt his body rising higher in the air while Anne seemed to fall away from him. Stars exploded in his field of vision as his head hit the roof, and then he was bouncing in his seat, the shoulder strap biting into his flesh even through his heavy coat. At some point, the airbags must have deployed, for the next time his head went forward, it slammed into a tough but yielding surface.

Then all was still. The last ringing sounds of the crash echoed away into silence, but as his scrambled senses began to find their focus, he detected a harsh, metallic clicking somewhere beyond the dashboard. A few seconds later, Anne groaned softly, followed by low stirrings from the backseat. He discovered, to his surprise, he was still sitting upright.

"Are we alive?" Kristin whispered.

"I'm pretty sure we're alive," came Roger's gruff voice.

"Anne?" Warren asked, a frigid wave of fear for her rushing over him. "You okay?"

For a long time, there was no response. Finally, her thin voice replied, "I think so. I can't tell."

He reached into the darkness toward her but then realized he was clutching something in his right hand: something cold, thin, and metallic. He felt the tiny ridged surfaces beneath his fingertips, and he knew immediately what the object was. He had no idea how it had gotten there. It had been in the back pocket of his jeans, and he knew—he *knew*—he had not reached into it and withdrawn the little engraved disk.

"Oh, God," he heard Kristin groan. "It's still out there. Whatever it is, it's still out there."

There was a long silence. Then, somewhere in the car, one of their phones began to ring.

Chapter Two
7:24 PM

Warren Burr, Anne Delmar, and the Levermans—Roger and Kristin—had driven up from Aiken Mill to Stonewall Chateau Restaurant and Winery, just off the Blue Ridge Parkway, for New Year's Eve dinner.

Severe snowstorms had swept through the week before Christmas, but the main roads to the chateau proved perfectly clear, and even here, at the crest of the ridge, only a thin layer of snow coated the ground. The sprawling, granite-sided building, with its high, sharply angled roof and vast porte cochere, resembled a huge stone church more than an actual chateau, but a galaxy of multicolored Christmas lights and a series of golden lanterns along the wooded path from the parking lot turned its austere façade distinctly festive. The building was less than three decades old, but it conveyed an aspect of historic grandeur that Warren appreciated. He had brought Anne here back in the summer, on her birthday. This was Roger and Kristin's first time.

"Hell of a lot colder up here," Roger grumbled, turning up his overcoat collar as they made haste for the main doors. Warren had to chuckle; if Roger wasn't bitching about something, Roger wasn't happy. He'd carried on so during the hour-long drive that Warren figured he must be ecstatic. Roger was only thirty—eighteen years Warren's junior—but well on his way to becoming a practiced curmudgeon.

Inside, the chateau's familiar, warm atmosphere immediately expelled the chill from Warren's bones, and a mélange of sweet scents—wood smoke, spices, and seared meat—reminded him that hunger was knocking at the door. To either side of the grand foyer, glittering beneath a crystal chandelier, two walls of wine bottles rose to the high ceiling. A handful of people, all smartly dressed, most holding drinks, milled about the bar area. His eyes found and lingered for a moment on a striking figure standing alone in a shadowed corner. It was a towering mountain of a man wearing a tailored black suit and a bowler hat that might have been fashionable early in the previous century, a glass of deep red wine in one hand, a ludicrously small, folded umbrella hanging from his other arm. Beneath the brim of the hat, his iron-gray hair was close-cropped, his pallid face clean shaven. A pair of very round, dark eyes swiveled toward Warren's, but before their gazes could meet, an attractive young brunette dressed in black greeted them and welcomed them to the chateau.

"We have a reservation," Warren said, his eyes wandering briefly back toward the spectacular giant. "Burr. Party of four."

"This way, please."

They followed the hostess, who led them past the bar, and for a moment, Warren felt the distinctive heat from a pair of eyes locking on the back of his head. He glanced back once and gave the man a brief, cold glare, hoping the other's gaze would falter. It did not. Then the hostess led them down a short hallway to the left and through two full dining rooms, to a cozy, fire-lit room with five tables, three of which were already occupied. Stonewall Chateau evidently drew a good crowd on New Year's Eve.

The low fire in the huge stone fireplace emitted little heat, but Anne pressed close to him, and he felt the warmth of her hand on the back of his. Just over a year ago, they both had divorced their spouses of many years and soon thereafter found each other—or rather, reunited with each other. Several years earlier, they had taught at the same high school and become close friends, at least until their jobs took them in different directions. Their respective marital situations, and their reasons for divorce, were very different, but the voids in their lives had been the same. At 36, Anne might be closer to Roger and Kristin's ages than his, but that fact mattered none at all, as they had discovered over the past several months. He had never felt so content with anyone. And she seemed genuinely happy—probably for the first time in her adult life, given all she had been through with her abusive ex-husband. She had married too young, he knew. Despite their deep commitment, neither had any abiding desire to marry the other, at least for the time being, and maybe they never would. And that was all right.

The fire, the candles on the table, and a dim chandelier above their table provided the only light in the dining room and, together with the exposed timbers and high rafters overhead, produced an almost medieval ambiance. Roger had taken to scowling at the wine list, though Warren knew that Roger enjoyed Stonewall's products maybe a little too much. The Levermans had moved in next door to him seven years ago, back when he and Elizabeth had a reasonably stable marriage. Early on, the younger couple had hit it off with Warren, though there had always been some tension with Elizabeth, whose moodiness—and eventual breakdown—had caused problems with just about all their friends. After Elizabeth had left and he began seeing Anne, Roger and Kristin welcomed her like a new member of their family. Roger was the golf pro at The Sycamores Country Club in Aiken Mill, and Kristin had just officially become a practicing psychiatrist. After so many years of school and struggling to make ends meet, she was finally racking up some billable hours, much to her husband's relief. Warren figured it would be entertaining to insist that she cover tonight's check, except for the fact she might actually do it.

Anne squeezed his hand, and he felt her gaze turning away from the table. In a very soft voice, she said, "Not to be mean, but that is *not* an example of a handsome human male."

He didn't even have to look up to understand. The air seemed to change, as if a dank, oppressive cloud had settled over the room, as the massive figure lumbered through the entryway. Hardly fair to prejudge the man, of course, but he bore such an unpleasant air, a demeanor that hinted at something more than eccentricity. His roaming eyes, when they settled, settled way too long and too intently for comfort. Warren waited for someone—anyone—else to appear to accompany him, but the hostess led him to the last vacant table, where he sat down alone.

"Enjoy your dinner, Mr. Hanger," the young woman said and whisked out of the dining room, her eyes making a brief contact with Warren's, as if to signal *caution*. Out of the corner of his eye, he watched Mr. Hanger remove his bowler hat and place it in the seat next to him. He unfolded his napkin fastidiously, but then shook it out with a flourish and laid it in his lap, watching his hands as if they were alien to him. His eyes began to rove around the room, and Warren lowered his to his menu just in time to avoid meeting the other's gaze. Anne, who had apparently watched the entire display, chuckled softly.

"You're playing a game with him."

"I am not. Just a little put out."

"He's not *that* offensive."

He gave her a weary look. "I was referring to the absence of wine at our table. We've been here more than three minutes. Quite intolerable."

Her eyes sparkled at him. "Mr. Patience."

As if on cue, their server, a blond, blue-eyed young man with an expression so dour as to make Warren think "Neue Hitler Youth," materialized next to Anne and took their drink orders with marked efficiency, but he cracked a slight smile when Roger glared at him and said, "I'll tell you up front. I like my wine red. Blood red. But I am going to order fish for dinner. Do not mock me when I place this order. Clear?"

"Very clear, sir."

Warren had chosen a bottle of Stonewall's Cabernet Franc, which he knew Anne would appreciate, and Roger and Kristin ordered the Petit Verdot. As the waiter hurried off toward the kitchen, Roger glared after him with an indignant expression.

"Did you see that? He was smirking. That rotten bastard."

"He was not," Kristin said.

"Yes, he was."

"No," she said. "I don't think that guy is capable of smirking."

"Maybe not," Roger conceded, "but I'm pretty sure I don't like him."

"Does it matter?"

"No."

Without thinking, Warren let his eyes drift toward Mr. Hanger's table, and to his dismay, he found himself the object of a deep, scrutinizing stare, and now there was nothing for it but to send the other a long, reproving glare. Finally, he put on a scowl worthy of Roger and averted his eyes—a clear enough signal, he hoped, that they did not appreciate the man's persistent gaze.

"Still staring," Anne said, very softly, and now Kristin and Roger had noticed that their table had become the focus of unwelcome attention.

Kristin leaned toward Anne and whispered, "That's not creepy, is it?"

"Not in the least. Except that it is."

"Can't say as I like him, either," Roger said, a little louder than necessary, and for a moment, Warren thought he might actually go over and confront Mr. Hanger, but just then, the very Aryan waiter returned to serve their wine and take their dinner orders, and all thoughts of the strange giant and his rude stares fled as the prospect of sating their hunger became their sole focus. From the start, veal saltimbocca and bison steak had been battling for Warren's favor, and by the slimmest margin, the bison steak won. Anne, however, went with the veal, and Roger and Kristin both ordered crabmeat-stuffed flounder. The wine, as always, proved excellent, and as it began to vanish at an alarming rate, Warren and Roger found themselves deriding each other for their respective choices of smart phone.

Anne's hand had been resting comfortably on his right thigh, her fingers occasionally moving to stroke the back of his hand or interlock with his fingers—her subtle and pleasurable way of conveying her affection—and he was so accustomed to her touch that he was scarcely aware of it. But full awareness returned abruptly when her fingers became rigid claws and dug into his leg, causing him to wince, and he turned toward her, only to freeze when he realized a massive shadow was creeping over their table.

"Good evening," said a low, mellifluous voice, tinged with some unidentifiable accent. "Forgive me for intruding."

The huge, black-suited figure had come to stand at the end of their table closest to Anne, and as all eyes turned to him, he bowed his head briefly and lifted one lip in what must have been his interpretation of a smile. Up close, his face appeared wan and rubbery, almost masklike. He clasped his hands in front of his massive belly, perhaps a gesture of humility. For a second, Warren felt a twinge of pity for the homely creature.

"You seem very pleasant young people," he said, glancing at Warren, who raised an eyebrow; he would have put the man at no older than fifty, probably a few years shy. "Allow me to introduce myself. My name is John Hanger. I wonder if I might have a few words with you."

Warren's guard immediately went up, and he saw Roger stiffen. "What about?"

"Matters of some importance. Do you come from nearby, may I ask?"

Before anyone else could speak, Warren said, "What exactly do you want, Mr. Hanger?"

The round, rather watery eyes fixed on him. "Like certain human beings, I have a clear purpose in life, and I am duty-bound to share that purpose with others. Perhaps you would say that it is my calling. Not to take much of your time, but I'm sure at least some of you might benefit from what I have to share."

"Let me guess," Roger said. "Jehovah's Witness, right? I've got to tell you, that's not earning you any points." He glanced at Kristin, who seemed to be listening intently to each word Hanger spoke.

"No, I'm not a Jehovah's Witness. Or a follower of any faith you would know. However, for our purposes, it would be fair to describe me as a missionary, of a kind."

"Mr. Hanger," Anne said, putting on her most diplomatic face, "I'm afraid we didn't come here for this kind of thing. And I don't think the restaurant manager would approve of you soliciting other guests."

His eyes rolled slowly toward Anne. "Soliciting? Oh, no. I am not asking you for anything, apart from a small amount of your time. A modest request, yes?"

Roger leaned forward, the rising blaze in his eyes a clear sign he was barely keeping his temper in check, but Kristin laid a calming hand on his wrist and said, "Why us, Mr. Hanger?"

A smile struggled back to his face. "I have the unique ability to take an accurate measure of individuals I encounter. And I actually surmised that you, in particular, might be receptive to my intentions."

"You are remarkably self-aware then. To recognize that characteristic in yourself."

Roger glanced at Warren and with a frown of exasperation nodded toward Kristin. "She would latch onto that, wouldn't she?" To her, he said, "You're not with a client, Curly-Q. No need to draw things out here."

"For example," Hanger said, ignoring Roger, "It is your way, I'm certain, to take the initiative, just as you have here, rather than be led."

"All right," Warren said, clapping one hand on the table. "Mr. Hanger, not to be rude, but I think we've made it clear that we're not here to be witnessed to, and we'd prefer to have our dinner without interruption. I hope we don't have to call the manager."

He gazed at Warren for an uncomfortably long time, frost gathering in his blue-gray irises. Finally, he offered them a curt bow. "I understand your reticence, sir. I had no intention of upsetting you or being a nuisance." He glanced at Kristin and then at Anne. "Perhaps I did misjudge at least some of you."

"Well, there's your uncanny personal measuring ability," Roger said, with a little snort. "Mr. Hanger, God invented church on Sunday for spreading the word. I've always found that to be more than adequate."

Hanger showed no sign that he had heard Roger, but returned his attention to Warren. "I will leave you. But before I do, please accept a small token from me. A parting gift." Without ceremony, he reached forward and laid on the table a shiny, gold-colored disk, about the size of a silver dollar but almost paper-thin, inscribed with an array of characters that, at first glance, appeared to be Japanese or Chinese. "I'm sure that in due time you will interpret its meaning. I bid you a pleasant evening." With that, he turned and strode back to his table, where he sat down and fixed his eyes on his glass of wine. He did not look back at them.

"The offender takes offense," Roger said with a sigh of contempt. "Something we said?"

"I don't think he heard a word *you* said," Kristin said, giving him a sidelong glance. "If only the rest of us could be so lucky."

"You always say you wish I would talk more."

"Meaningfully. Talk meaningfully. You, with me."

"What do you call this?"

"Noise."

Warren picked up the disk, its polished surface catching the light of the candles as if it were a golden mirror. He glanced over at Hanger, who appeared to be devoting all his energy to ignoring them. The engraved characters, which covered both sides of the disk, were not Asian after all, but geometric figures composed of intricate angles and curves. He had no idea what they represented, if anything. Anne pressed close to him, peering at the object with a thoughtful frown.

"Know what these mean?" he asked.

She shook her head. "Looks like they're supposed to be words or syllables. See how some of them are repeated?"

"Some kind of code?" Kristin asked.

"A code," Anne said, nodding. "Could be a code, I guess."

"Could be bullshit," Roger offered.

"Yes," Kristin said without looking at him, leaning over the table to peer at the disk. "That would explain it, wouldn't it?"

"Why don't you just wander over there and ask him?"

"That's probably just what he wants," Anne said, giving the perfectly oblivious Hanger a quick glance. To him, they apparently no longer existed.

They pondered the markings on the disk a few minutes more, quite in vain, and when the very blond waiter arrived with their entrees, Warren slipped the object into his back pocket, where it remained, all but forgotten, for the rest of their meal. The bison steak—perfectly medium rare and brushed with a red wine and olive oil sauce—convinced him that he had made the right choice, but when Anne offered him a sampling of her veal, he decided that it would have been just as satisfying. The wine, as well, could hardly have made him happier, and it wasn't until they had finished the last glass that he glanced up and saw that Mr. Hanger was gone. It seemed he should have noticed the big man getting up to leave, but he had been too focused on his dinner and his company. He shrugged to himself; why should it even matter? Somehow, though, the fact that Hanger had departed unseen left him feeling unsettled.

Anne saw him staring at the space Hanger had vacated. "That was not a pleasant man," she said. "Kind of scary."

"The hostess thought so too," Kristin said. "Did you notice when he came in?"

Anne shook her head, but Warren said, "I did. Still, you can't condemn someone just for being peculiar."

"That's some kind of peculiar," Roger grumbled.

A gentle pattering of percussion and a chorus of bells, like wind chimes, rose gradually, and Warren realized it was his phone ringing. He took it from his jacket pocket and checked the caller ID, only to find no number showing on the display—just a series of glowing geometric figures, composed of complex angles and curves.

"Now, *that* is messed up," he said, and held up the phone so Anne could see the screen.

"What on earth?"

He turned the display to Roger and Kristin, who gaped in surprise, and then pressed the answer key. "Yes?"

No voice came from the other end of the line; only a quavering, high-pitched tone—something between a moan and a whistle—with a hollow timbre, as if it originated from some vast distance. He looked at the screen again. To his surprise, the activity icon at the top of the screen indicated something was installing itself on his phone. A few seconds later, a new image had formed: an array of the strange geometric figures, glowing pale green against a black background, surrounding a row of ten white boxes, each slightly larger than the individual characters.

"What the hell?"

Anne was peering over his shoulder. "It looks like you're supposed to move the characters into those boxes."

"Is it some kind of game?" Kristin asked, leaning partway over the table.

Anne shook her head. "I don't think so."

"It's not a game," Warren said thoughtfully. He noticed the quavering tone had fallen silent, and the characters glowed like fiery green embers in expectant silence. "This is messed up."

"You got hacked," Roger said, craning his neck for a moment, just long enough to get a glimpse of the display. "That would never happen on *my* phone."

Warren put a finger to the screen and touched one of the

characters. It vibrated beneath his fingertip. "Sure enough, they move," he said.

"It is a puzzle of some kind," Kristin said. "It must be."

"Try moving one of the characters into a box," Anne said.

He touched one of the glowing figures and slid his finger toward the first white box. The character moved with it, but then bounced back to its original position as soon as he released it. "Wait a minute," he said, remembering the disk in his pocket. He dug it out and held it up next to his phone to examine the engravings. On one side, in the center of the disk, there were ten figures in a row. He searched the glowing shapes for one that matched the first character on the disk. When he found it, he slid it into the first box, where it changed to blood red and remained.

"That's it," Anne said. "Now, just move the matching figures into the boxes."

"There, there's the second one," Kristin said with some excitement, as if she had discovered the key to winning a high-stakes game. She reached across the table and pointed to the display. "And the next one."

One by one, Warren moved the characters into the boxes in the same order as those on the disk. As he slid the final character into its box, he felt a thrill of both satisfaction and strange apprehension, unsure what to expect—if he had indeed solved the puzzle. For all he knew, it might be some bug that would steal or wipe out all the data on his phone. Clearly, John Hanger was responsible. But he couldn't have known Warren's name, much less his phone number. And how the hell could he have remotely installed and activated some unknown app?

For several long moments, nothing happened. Stationary, the red figures glowed in their boxes, and the phone's speaker remained silent. Perhaps he hadn't solved the puzzle correctly after all. Or nothing was meant to happen. He felt the others' eyes on the screen, the air of expectant tension almost corporeal.

Finally, very slowly, the white boxes began to dissolve, until only the red figures remained, burning like hot coals against the black background. Behind them, a misty, indistinct shape began to form, like a gray cloud in a midnight sky, and the figures started to move, shaping themselves into a jagged circle, which whirled into motion to become a spinning, blazing buzz saw blade in the center of the screen. In the background, the gray cloud pulsated like something alive, and for a second, Warren swore he glimpsed a reddish-gold globe, almost like an eyeball, emerge from the center of the roiling mass, which had acquired a semblance of depth and dimension, as if the flat display were a window to some vast space beyond. Before the bright globe vanished, it seemed to radiate *sentience*, giving him the impression some unknown intelligence had actually recognized him. He felt himself jerk back in his chair, his nerves jangling.

"What's the matter?" Anne asked, concern in her eyes.

He shook his head. "I've just never seen anything like this."

"What about the disk itself?" Kristin asked. "Could it be affecting your phone somehow?"

"No way," Anne said, giving the gleaming disk a long, dubious look. "No way that's some electronic gadget."

"It's not," Warren said, but he glanced at the disk and began to wonder. What else *could* explain it? He took the object from the table and ran his fingers over its cold, engraved surface. No; it was just a piece of inert metal.

At last, the jagged, whirling circle on the screen began to fade, and the undulating cloud vanished into the black backdrop. The display reverted to its customary, aquatic-themed background and array of icons, appearing as if nothing out of the ordinary had ever happened—though he realized that the back of the phone had grown hot, almost scorching. He placed it on the table and gave it a long, wary stare. "This is all kinds of messed up."

Roger held up his own phone, waved it back and forth a few times, and gave Warren a smug grin.

"Is that it?" Anne asked. "What did it mean?"

'It means I should know better than to play around with strange apps," Warren said, thoroughly frustrated with himself.

"You ought to dump everything and do a system restore," Roger said. "No telling what kind of bug you've got on there now."

"Mr. Hanger must be one clever fellow. I'd like to know how he managed that. Whatever *that* was."

"We are just assuming it was him," Kristin said, looking at the empty chair where he had sat.

"Those figures from the disk," Anne said. "It *had* to be his doing."

"Almost makes you wish we had actually let him talk with us," Roger said.

"I don't know that I would go that far," Anne said.

"I would," Warren said, staring at his phone. "He's probably an identity thief."

"But he doesn't even know who we are," Kristin said.

"I wouldn't bet on that," Roger said. "Clever, rotten bastard."

"I made our reservations online. If he got hold of the restaurant's reservations list, it would have my contact information on it," Warren said.

Roger nodded. "And now he's probably snagged all kinds of data from you."

"With a puzzle?" Kristin asked. "Seems like a roundabout way of doing it."

"Just a ploy. It would have ended the same no matter what we did."

"Perhaps," Warren said, looking around for their young waiter, "I should have a chat with the manager."

Chapter Three
9:34 PM

The shrill ringtone filled the interior of the Pathfinder like a frantic scream.

"Not mine," Warren said, groping in his coat pocket for his phone.

"Mine," Roger said. He withdrew his phone, glanced at the display, and looked back up with an expression of shock. "The same thing. Those weird characters."

"Don't answer it," Kristin said.

He gazed at Warren. "Do I?"

"He might have gotten my number from the reservation list. But not yours."

"Then how the hell can he be calling my phone?"

"Do *not* answer it," Kristin said again. She peered out the window into the darkness. "Listen. Don't you hear that? Whatever it is out there, it's coming again."

Anne cocked her head to listen. "I do."

Roger seemed to make up his mind. He touched the "answer" button and said into the mic, "Are you there, you son of a bitch?"

As with Warren's phone earlier, the speaker emitted only a whistling tremolo tone. And on the display, rather than forming a puzzle, the brilliant figures immediately arranged themselves into a wheel and began to spin. He pressed and held the power switch, but the phone refused to shut off.

"Damn it, Roger," Kristin groaned, but now the heavy booming sounds—still distant but clearly moving closer—had captured her full attention. "We can't stay in here," she said.

"Agreed," Warren said. "This could be a deathtrap."

"But where do we go?" Anne asked, her eyes widening with dread. "We don't even know for sure where we are."

"It's a long way back to where we came from," Roger said. "I didn't see a single house or light along the road."

"I don't think it matters now. Let's move." Warren shoved his door open, and Anne managed to clamber out on the passenger side with some difficulty. Kristin pushed hard against her door, but it wouldn't budge, either jammed from the tumble down the hill or wedged against a tree. Roger deftly opened the door on his side, grabbed Kristin's hand, and pulled her into the frigid darkness behind him.

"Come on, Curly-Q."

As Warren slid from his seat, cold wind slapped his face like a gigantic, icy hand, shocking in its brutality. It had been *nothing* like this up at the chateau. For a few seconds, he crouched behind his open door, using it to block the wind, wondering whether it might be wiser to stay inside the Pathfinder. But no; soon it would be just as cold inside as out, and if someone did drive past, they'd never see the vehicle, fifty feet below the road and half-buried in the snow.

Whatever was making those heavy sounds was still coming closer.

Trees falling, from the ice and snow and wind. It had to be.

But so rhythmic. So continuous. Something was knocking the trees down.

Something huge.

Anne came trudging around the vehicle, awkward in her high-heeled dress boots, keeping her balance with one gloved hand on the hood. Warren took her hand and pointed up the steep hillside. "We have to get back up to the road."

She nodded grimly. "I can do that."

"No problem," Roger said, giving Kristin a concerned glance. "We've got to do it. You okay?"

"I'll make it."

A torrent of tinny percussion and plinking keyboards rang out from somewhere nearby, and Anne touched her coat pocket. "My phone."

"Leave it be," Kristin said. "This time, really, just leave it be."

Anne nodded but withdrew her phone and looked at the display. "The same characters." Hers was an older phone, but on the small, inch-square window on the back of the flip top, the bizarre characters had already formed themselves into a whirling spiral. "It can't do that," she said, looking up at Warren. "It just can't."

"It doesn't matter whether you answer or not," Warren said. "He's got us tracked somehow."

"All it took was one," Roger said, nodding. "Once you solved the puzzle, he had us."

Warren took out his own phone and looked at it warily, almost afraid to try using it. One bar out of four on the display. He entered 911 on the dialer.

Nothing. Nothing but dead silence.

"You didn't expect anything different, did you?" Roger asked.

"Not really, no."

Kristin's phone rang.

As the blazing red characters on her display formed a jagged circle and began to spin, a deep, heavy *boom* came from somewhere shockingly nearby, and a flurry of snow and ice crystals swirled down from the trees like a miniature blizzard.

"It's right on us," Roger said, craning his neck to peer up toward the road.

"What do we do?" Anne asked.

He peered down the hill at the thick woods and then back up the steep slope. "Change of plan. Stay put. At least for the moment."

Warren felt a vibration beneath his feet: the ground trembling as if a fault line had shifted—or some unimaginable giant had taken a step toward them. A frigid breeze swept over his face, carrying with it the taint of something fetid. *The giant's breath*, he thought.

"Come here," he said, reaching for Anne's hand. He took it and pulled her toward him. "Get down. Everybody, get down."

He let his body collapse next to the Pathfinder, his arms around Anne and pulling her with him. A few feet away, near the front of the vehicle, Roger and Kristin knelt in the snow, and he pulled her close and covered her with his body. They huddled against the still-warm metal, making themselves as small as possible, keenly aware of the approach of something deadly.

Looking up, he saw it: a mass of billowing gray cloud, rolling slowly across the starless black sky until it settled directly over them—too deliberate, too calculated, to be random. In its boiling heart, something flashed, and Warren realized it was like the image that had appeared on his phone's display. A second later, a reddish, cyclopean eye opened to gaze down at them, and though he had seen it once before, the sight of it wrenched the breath from his lungs and sent him toppling into the snow.

✷

Chapter Four
8:54 PM

"**I** am Mr. Fothering," the gray-haired, bespectacled, rather emaciated-looking gentleman said, his soft voice almost breathless, as if he suffered from acute asthma. "You were inquiring about Mr. John Hanger, I believe?"

"Yes," Warren said.

"He's something of a regular. Dines here at least once every season. And almost always on New Year's Eve."

"And you've never had any complaints about him?" Warren asked.

Fothering's eyes batted back and forth nervously. "Can't say that we have. Granted, he's something of an odd duck. Usually keeps to himself, though."

"Not tonight, he didn't," Roger said.

"How long has he been coming here?"

Fothering stroked his chin. "Six or seven years. Always orders the same thing—roast pork and a bottle of our Reserve Tannat."

"Could he have gotten hold of your reservations list?" Roger asked, giving the older man a piercing glare.

"No, not at all. It's on our computer, anyway."

Roger's eyes lit up, and he looked at Warren. "He's a hacker. That's got to be it."

"Why single us out?" Kristin asked.

"Had to be somebody. Why not us?"

"But why would he come talk to us? And give us that disk?"

"Why do some people marry their high school girlfriends, Kit Kat? Because they're all messed up."

"And you base these suppositions on a phone call?" Fothering peered at them over the top of his glasses, one eye still twitching back and forth.

Warren held the engraved disk out to the older man. "Ever see this before? Or anything like it?"

Fothering bent forward and studied the odd geometric characters. He hesitated for a moment, then shook his head. "No. What is it?"

With as much patience as he could muster, Warren explained Hanger's attempt to engage them, his presenting the disk to them, and the subsequent anomaly on his phone. "As you can see, it can't be a coincidence."

"No, that doesn't seem likely," Fothering said with a resigned shrug. "But what do you want me to do about it?"

"You have contact information for him?" Roger asked. "Address? Phone number?"

The old man scowled. "Oh, no, I don't have any of his personal information. Even if I did, I couldn't just let you have it."

"You realize he may have committed a crime on your property, right?" Anne said, giving Fothering her sternest teacher's glare.

"But you don't know that he actually did anything at all—other than send you a puzzle game on your telephone."

"He didn't just ring me up because we're old friends,"

Warren said dryly. "Clearly, he hacked my phone, after he made a nuisance of himself in your establishment."

"I'm very sorry about that. But I really don't know how else I might help you." Fothering threw a suspicious glance at Warren. "I must tell you, if you're looking to get a free meal, I'm afraid—"

"No, no," Warren said, holding up a hand, resigned to the fact they would get nothing further from the manager. "Dinner was fine. We are satisfied."

Fothering's nervous eyes brightened with some relief. "Thank you. I'll do this. One of your bottles of wine is complimentary. On the house. For your trouble."

"That's very kind," Anne said, glancing at Warren. "But it really isn't necessary."

"Forget it," Warren said to the old man. "We're not looking to get something for free."

"I'm relieved to hear that," Fothering said, one eye warming to them, the other still cold. "Truly, I am sorry you were inconvenienced."

"I'm not sure 'inconvenienced' is the word for it," Roger grumbled.

"I think we're done," Kristin said softly to him. She smiled at Fothering and nodded toward Roger. "He's really a sweetheart."

"I'm sure."

They left the front desk and headed toward the main doors, Fothering gazing after them with a thoughtful, if dismayed expression. Roger turned to Warren. "You know what I think?"

"That he knows John Hanger better than he lets on?"

Roger nodded in satisfaction. "Yep."

"Oh, I don't think so," Kristin said, frowning at Roger.

"Yes," Anne said. "They're right. Didn't you notice his

eyes? I bet others have complained about Mr. Hanger, but Mr. Fothering doesn't care to do anything about it."

"Why would he not?"

"You're the psychiatrist, Karla Jung."

"He's afraid," Anne said.

"Yes," Warren said. "That seemed pretty obvious to me. There's something else. A little thing, but it made me wonder."

"What?"

"Fothering said John Hanger always orders roast pork. Did you see roast pork on tonight's menu?"

"Come to think of it, no," Roger said. "They had bison, beef, chicken, veal, venison, lamb, and all kinds of seafood, but there was no roast pork."

"Maybe they do it specially for Mr. Hanger," Kristin said.

"I'm guessing not."

"Well, I'll tell you what. We can brood on this all night without a resolution, or we can head back home and celebrate New Year's like we had planned."

"Good point," Anne said.

"Yeah," Warren said, holding up his phone and gazing at it. "I'll do a system restore and hopefully it'll get rid of anything Hanger put on here."

"And keep an eye on your personal data."

They stepped out through the front doors to the shelter of the porte cochere. A light, chilly breeze crept out of the darkness, sending a thin mist of snow swirling in from the surrounding evergreen trees. Beyond the dark, spindly towers, the sky was clear, and Warren could see a few stars sparkling above the black crests of the nearby mountains. It was an hour's drive back home, and they planned to kill perhaps another bottle of wine at the Leverman's place before breaking out the champagne at midnight. Certainly, better to enjoy their evening together than dwell on the potential harm caused by a bizarre and evidently tech-savvy stranger.

He felt Anne's fingers take hold of his hand, and she leaned toward him and kissed his ear. "Dinner was fantastic. Let's enjoy the rest of the night."

"Done."

Yet, once into the Pathfinder and back on the Parkway, heading for the connector to Route 67 and Aiken Mill, they remained mostly silent—all still feeling a bit rattled. Though Warren hardly knew the ins and outs of hacking technology, it seemed beyond unlikely that John Hanger could have somehow installed an unknown app on his phone. Had he targeted them to begin with, or simply retaliated for their being rude to him? Surely the former, Warren thought, if he had swiped Warren's personal information from the restaurant's reservations list,

On the way up from Aiken Mill, the few miles they had traveled on the Blue Ridge Parkway had been mostly clear of snow and ice, but now, he began to see black, slick-looking patches that appeared fresh, despite the fact there had been no further inclement weather all evening and no new precipitation in the forecast. But the snow on either side of the road looked much deeper than it had on the trip up.

"This isn't good," Anne said, peering out at the deepening snow banks. "Slow down some, okay?"

He chuckled. Anne always mistrusted other people's driving—specifically his—even though she was the one with a pair of speeding tickets from the past year, and his driving record was near-perfect. "Fear not, young American woman, for I am not late for a hair appointment."

She gave him a withering glare, but it quickly melted into an abashed grin. "That's mean."

"But apt."

"Whoa," Roger said suddenly, leaning forward in his

seat, and Warren saw it at the same time: a white, sprawling blanket of snow and ice covering the road ahead, extending beyond the limit of his headlights' beams. He pressed the brakes gingerly, knowing he was going too fast, in spite of Anne's admonition—but he hadn't expected anything like this. That patch sure as hell hadn't been here on the way up. The Pathfinder slowed obediently, and clambered onto the layer of ice without sliding. Warren brought the SUV to a full stop and looked around, barely able to accept what he was seeing. The snow beside the road had to be every bit of two feet deep. Had a veritable blizzard moved through the area in the past hour, and somehow utterly missed the chateau? It was the only explanation.

"No comprendez," Roger said, staring out his window in disbelief. "We are going back the same way we came, right?"

"Yes, we are," Warren said. "Should be about a mile to Willis Road."

In the backseat, Roger took out his phone and tapped the local weather icon. "'Cannot load weather information,' it says. Now, there's a crock of shit."

Warren shifted into four-wheel drive and started forward again. There were no ruts in the ice and snow, no sign that any other vehicle had passed through the new accumulation. Anne reached forward and turned on the dashboard radio. After a few seconds' delay, a crash of harsh electronic noise erupted from the speakers, like a million crickets screeching in a dissonant chorus. Anne quickly lowered the volume and hit the seek button. The numbers on the digital display scurried up the scale but refused to lock on a station. Warren reached over and pressed a few of the preset keys. Nothing but static.

"It just gets happier and happier."

Warren kept the Pathfinder moving at a slow but steady speed. He'd driven this way many times, and he knew the

Parkway remained relatively straight and level until the turn-off at Willis Road. Or so he thought. The curves were becoming sharper, the trees pressing closer on either side. Even in four-wheel drive, the tires occasionally spun as they met patches of exposed ice. Then he hit the brakes, bringing the vehicle to a long, sliding halt. He switched on the GPS on his phone, and waited for the road map to appear on the display, unable to process what he was seeing beyond the windshield.

Somewhere in the distance, something crashed. He couldn't tell from which direction it came, but it was heavy and jarring—like a massive tree falling across the road.

"I don't know how or why," he said, looking from the map on his phone display to the narrow, winding corridor of snow-blanketed trees that descended at a shocking angle into unbroken darkness, "but we are sure as hell not on the Parkway anymore."

Chapter Five
9:44 PM

The sudden, blinding flash in the sky turned the landscape brilliant red for several seconds, leaving a vivid afterimage in Warren's vision even as darkness again settled over the woods. *An explosion,* he thought, and with nerves raw and jangling he waited for the deafening blast to pummel them, but nothing came—only the low moan of the wind, rising and falling like a siren. But then something blacker than black, like a negative image of a lightning bolt, hurtled out of the sky toward the earth, appearing to strike in the woods somewhere beyond the road. For a second, he thought he heard a hissing, sizzling sound, but then it gave way to the low moan of the wind. Anne's arms had constricted around his chest, but as the darkness deepened, she loosened her hold and fearfully raised her eyes to the sky. The cyclopean eye had vanished.

Her hand closed on his. "What the hell is happening?"

"I saw a weather balloon explode once," Kristin said. "It was kind of like that."

"That was no weather balloon," Anne whispered.

"That was nothing natural," Roger said, getting to his

feet and pulling Kristin up beside him. He gave Warren a long look. "You said it earlier. This is messed up. Really messed up."

"What was making those sounds? Was it *that*?" Anne pointed at the sky.

"We'd better try to get back up to the road," Warren said, anxious to divert their attention—including his own—from the thing in the sky. "Question is, do we head in the direction we've been going or try to go back? It's a lot of miles the way we came."

"At least we know what's back there," Kristin said. "We could have just as many miles ahead, or more." She was wearing a long, belted coat, but beneath it, only a short dress and flat-heeled boots. She was going to get very cold if they didn't reach safety soon.

Roger had activated his phone's GPS and was staring in disbelief at the screen. "According to this, we're absolutely nowhere." He held it up to Warren. The map no longer even showed the road. When he zoomed out, the display went blank. "Try yours."

Warren's phone gave him the same result.

"Not much battery power left."

"Can't we charge them in the car?"

Warren shook his head grimly. The cigarette lighter fuse in the Pathfinder had blown a while back, and changing it hadn't been high on his list of priorities.

More fool me.

"I still had service a couple of miles back. Not sure that means anything now." He turned to Anne. "How about yours?"

"Low. And no service."

"Same here," Kristin said. "But he called. John Hanger called us right here."

"Let's turn the phones off. Conserve power till we get to where we have service," Roger said.

"Agreed."

Even though his phone was no more useful than a hunk of ice at the moment, shutting it off felt like severing a lifeline. He dropped it into his inside coat pocket and turned to look at his wrecked Pathfinder. The front end was smashed against a tree, and the left front tire protruded at ninety degrees—the axle had broken. Despite knowing it could have been much worse, he felt a pang of bitterness. At least none of them had been seriously injured. He found himself glancing upward, barely able to avert his mind's eye from the nightmarish thing they'd seen in the sky. "Let's get everything out of there we might use. I've got a couple of flashlights. Bungee cords." He chuckled mirthlessly. "Golf clubs."

"Any flares?" Roger asked. "Fire might come in handy."

"Afraid not."

They gathered what remained of their belongings. In the glove compartment, along with his flashlights, Warren found a couple of packs of matches and a small toolkit with several screwdrivers, a wrench, and pair of pliers. On a whim, he stuffed the kit in his coat pocket. Then he opened the back and gathered a few coiled bungee cords. He handed one of the flashlights to Roger.

"Let's do this. It's not going to get any warmer."

Warren took hold of Anne's hand and started up the steep embankment. Thank God, he'd worn casual clothes, including his sturdy, thick-soled work boots. The snow reached almost to his knees, higher in places. Anne was struggling to keep moving in her high-heeled boots, but at least she had good balance and strong legs. He found that if he went up sideways, planting each boot firmly in the snow, he could maintain his footing, but the hill was growing steeper as he drew nearer the top. A few feet from the crest, one foot slid out from under him, and he went down, pulling Anne with him. He grabbed the base of a small tree to keep from sliding down the hill, but Anne lost her grip on his hand and slid several feet before she could stop herself.

"You're okay," Roger said, coming up behind her and helping her back upright. "Grab that tree right there and pull yourself around to Warren's right. Leave it to him to find the most difficult path."

She took Roger's advice and was able to use the branches of several small trees to pull herself up the embankment. At the crest, a tangle of vines and brambles protruded from the snow, and Warren grabbed hold of a cluster of vines, dug his feet into the thick brush, and dragged himself upward until he reached level ground. He turned around just in time to grab Anne's outstretched hand and pull her up beside him. Roger and Kristin followed moments later.

Warren's eyes sought the deep rut the Pathfinder had cut down the hillside, and when he saw from this perspective how steep the embankment was—and how far they'd tumbled—his heart slammed against the walls of his chest. Through a lattice of branches, he could make out only a trace of dark metal against the snow far below. It was a wonder any of them were still alive. And the SUV was almost assuredly down there for good.

"Good God," Anne whispered, standing beside him. "We were lucky."

He nodded and then turned toward the road, still uncertain which direction to take. Unless help came along, which seemed unlikely, it was a good eight or nine miles back to the chateau. If they continued in the direction they'd been going, they might find human habitation around the next bend, or—just as likely—twice as far ahead as they had already come.

He could not fathom how he had inadvertently turned off the Parkway.

"I say we keep going," Roger said. "This road has to lead somewhere."

"We're still halfway up the mountain," Kristin reminded him. "Hardly anyone lives up here."

"At least this way leads down. To get to Stonewall, we'd have to go back up and over."

"But we know it connects with the Parkway. Somewhere back there." She gave Warren a look that suggested she half-blamed him for their predicament.

"Best to go down," Warren said. "The lower altitude may be a little warmer, too."

"I agree," Anne said, though she gave Kristin an apologetic glance, as if she were less certain than she tried to sound.

"All right," Kristin said with a shrug. "Whichever, let's get moving. I'd rather not freeze to death here." Then her eyes flickered toward the sky, and Warren couldn't help but glance up at the vacant black canopy as well. It wasn't freezing to death at the root of their fear.

Some natural phenomenon. It had *to have been.*

"Let's move."

The ice-coated asphalt was too treacherous to walk on—the last thing they needed was for one of them to be injured in a fall—so they set out along the side of the road, trudging through ankle-deep snow. With no moon to illuminate the way, it was agonizingly slow going. Warren didn't want to use the flashlights unless it became absolutely necessary, for the batteries were anything but fresh. Numerous times, black tree limbs appeared right in front of him, and briers occasionally reached out from beneath the innocuous-looking, soft white cover to snag his clothing.

Just keep going, one step at a time. We can all use the exercise after a dinner like that.

"Listen," Anne said, coming up beside him. "Is that a train?"

Warren paused and cocked his head, thinking he had indeed heard a distant ringing and rumbling. It was hard to discern over the moaning wind, but he could make out a deep, almost eerie throbbing that must have been a train somewhere far below. Impossible to guess how far away it was. He found it strangely comforting to hear something of distinctly human origin. Quite the opposite of his typical sentiments, he thought wryly.

They hadn't gone much farther when they noticed the ice on the road ahead looked dull and rough; the asphalt was giving way to gravel, Warren realized. His heart sank, for he had dared hope the road would improve as they made their way toward lower altitudes. No one said anything, but he perceived a subtle change in the air, which told him the others more than shared his frustration.

Now the road was descending into a new lightless pit, and as they proceeded, the darkness became so overwhelming that Warren finally pulled the flashlight from his pocket and aimed it into the abyss. Roger evidently had the same idea, for a second later, the beam of his light joined Warren's, and then the four of them came to an abrupt halt.

Before them, the road vanished. Their lights fell upon a solid wall of giant poplars and pines, their trunks girdled with spindly boughs of mountain laurel. Warren could only stand and gape dumbly at the barricade, hot anger surging through his system. He heard Kristin hiss in fury, and he felt certain it was at least partially directed at him. Beside him, Anne simply sighed in disappointment and placed a gentle hand on his shoulder. He laid one hand on hers to show his appreciation.

"Good for nothing piece of shit bitch, you've got to be fucking kidding me." Roger spat into the snow beside the road.

"Well," Anne said, taking a deep, steadying breath. "We go back."

"Yeah," Roger growled, shining his light around at the woods, as if convinced the road must yet continue somewhere. "We go back."

They turned, but Warren hesitated. Why on earth would a road lead this far into the woods only to end up absolutely nowhere? No houses, no farmland, no nothing. Just a long, empty, pointless road.

Anne was obviously thinking the same thing. "It's an old road. Maybe people lived up here, a lot of years ago."

"But not anymore."

"Wait," Kristin said, looking back toward the barricade of trees. "Shine your light down there again."

"Why?"

"I think I saw something."

Warren focused the light on the trees in the direction she was pointing, and then he noticed something glittering in the darkness—something bright red. For a chilling second, it brought to mind the cyclopean eye that had appeared in the sky, until he determined it must be something metal. He made his way into the trees, holding his flashlight beside his head at eye level, fixing the shining object with his beam.

"Oh, my God," Anne whispered, already realizing what they were seeing. The shock hit Warren at the same moment.

It was a polished, copper-colored disk, like the one John Hanger had given him, attached to the trunk of a huge poplar, a foot or so above their heads. Warren could make out the strange geometric figures engraved on its surface, identical— or at least similar—to those on the disk in his pocket. As he studied it more closely, he realized the disk did not appear to be bolted or otherwise affixed to the tree; it looked more like a material part of the trunk, with bark growing around it.

"Fucked. Up." Roger said.

"This can't be a coincidence. It can't," Kristin said.

"I don't like it," Anne said softly, so only Warren could hear. "Feels like someone's out here watching us."

"John Hanger?"

"Maybe."

He sent his flashlight beam roving through the woods, seeking any sign of movement, human or otherwise. He could hear only the wind in the trees, but, like Anne, he felt certain that someone or something was watching them. He almost wished John Hanger *were* out here, for he—and Roger—would certainly leave the big man with some unpleasant memories to reflect upon. But whatever peculiar sensation he felt, it wasn't John Hanger's gaze. "We should get moving," he said. "Right now."

Roger shot him a curious look; then his gaze went past him, into the woods, and he nodded. He took hold of Kristin's hand. "Yeah, let's go."

They switched off their lights and started walking back the way they had come, all keeping very close together. Warren leaned toward Roger. "You see something back there?"

"Something shiny."

They picked up the pace a little, as much as they could in the snow, which now seemed even deeper and heavier than it had only minutes before. A couple of times, Warren thought he heard a distant but sharp crackling sound somewhere in the woods, and he found his eyes repeatedly delving into the black spaces beyond the nearest trees rather than where he was going. He stumbled and nearly pitched headlong, but Anne's grip on his arm kept him from going all the way down.

"Thanks."

"We should have reached the asphalt by now," she said. "Why aren't we back on the paved road?"

"That's what I was just thinking," Roger said.

"And we're going downhill," Kristin said, her voice getting shrill. "Going the other way, we didn't go uphill. Not once."

Anne jerked to a halt, nearly pulling Warren off balance. "No, we didn't." He felt her eyes burning into his. "What is going on? How can this be happening?"

He shook his head, fighting down panic, keener and deeper than any he'd ever known. "Just keep walking. We were just too rattled to notice. We were in a hell of a car wreck."

Anne nodded, and he knew she desperately wanted to accept his explanation yet couldn't. But there *was* no other explanation. He had to cling to it. They all did.

"I'm so damned cold," Kristin said. Roger pulled her closer to him.

They had only taken a few more steps when Warren heard it again: a distinct sizzling sound, like flames in the forest. But there was no hint of light amid the trees. Something moving through the snow-covered underbrush? A large animal, maybe? Surely, not a bear, not this time of year.

Just keep going.

One step after another, and Warren realized the cold was working its way into his bones. So far, his exertions had kept warmth flowing through his body, but how long could they continue like this? If they stopped to rest, the cold would attack them with renewed ferocity. Eventually, it would overcome them.

They should have reached the wrecked Pathfinder by now. But the road had yet to begin ascending again. And beneath the ice, it was still gravel.

Ahead, the blackness appeared denser, more overwhelming than before. He wanted to avoid using the flashlight, to conserve the batteries, but he withdrew it from his pocket, switched it on, and aimed its beam into the black barrier ahead.

"God, no."

The beam from Roger's flashlight joined his, and they weaved back and forth, illuminating the harsh, impossible reality confronting them.

The road ended at another impenetrable wall of trees.

They must have gotten turned around and headed right back where they had come from.

But they hadn't. *They hadn't.*

"This can't be," Anne whispered.

"Just like we never turned off the Parkway," Roger said. "And look where we've ended up. We're prisoners."

"The land itself is changing," Anne said. "That's the only explanation."

Kristin's eyes blazed at her. "You don't know what you're saying."

"Do you think we got turned around somehow? How did we get off the Parkway? We didn't make a single turn."

"What else could have happened? We *must* have gotten turned around."

"What about that thing in the sky? We all saw it. What do you think that was?"

Kristin's eyes gleamed with panic, her inability to process what was happening to them. "So what does it mean? Are we dead? Is that it?"

"We're not fucking dead," Roger said.

She looked on the verge of bursting into tears. Warren wouldn't have expected Kristin to be the one overcome with emotion. Ordinarily, her demeanor was clinical, even detached, suited to her profession. But she was so young. And this situation being what it was…*whatever* it was…who knew how any of them would react?

As he looked around, he noticed a brilliant, copper-colored point of light amid the trees ahead. He pointed it out to Roger. "No surprise anymore, is it?"

"Wouldn't know what to expect otherwise."

Anne's fingers became claws around his wrist. "There's something in the woods."

Warren nodded. "I heard it a ways back. Do you see anything?"

She shook her head. "Sounded like flames. Like a big fire."

"That's what I thought too."

Then, above the wind, he heard it again. They all stood motionless, as if ice had encased their feet. And then again: a hissing, popping, rumbling sound, like a firestorm rushing toward them through the trees. Yet the woods remained a chasm of unbroken black shadow, swallowing even the white expanse of snow. Warren felt a tug on his arm and heard Anne whisper, "Come on. Let's not stay here."

"Where are we going?"

"Anywhere."

For a second, he glimpsed a bluish light, just a quick flash, some distance ahead. Then it came again, casting dim illumination on the trees, the harsh sound rising—definitely moving closer. His heart clanged like a sledgehammer on iron, shutting out all other sound, but curiosity now wrangled with his rising fear, the urge to *see* the approaching unknown almost overpowering. Anne tugged at him again, her instincts urging her only to flee. He stood rooted to the spot, knowing there was nowhere to run, for yes, the land *was* changing around them, and even if they followed the road, it would end again, somehow at the behest of the stranger, John Hanger. He would bet their lives on it.

"There," Roger said, his eyes fixed on a patch of darkness just beyond the nearest scraggly pines. "I saw it. Damn, I saw it."

"What?" Kristin asked, her voice quavering. "What is it?"

"Don't move," Roger said. "Whatever you do, don't move."

The sharp, electrical crackling sound that tore itself from the darkness was like a livewire spitting raw energy. And then the thing was rushing toward them: a living ball of black lightning, a compact, writhing mass of electricity—in negative—twisting, arcing, dancing amid the knotted pine boughs. It gave off no light except for the blue-black pulsing of several luminous, antennae-like tendrils that flickered from its periphery, all curling in and out of the nearby trees, as if the thing were feeling its way toward them through the forest. Just before coming fully into view, the animated black mass halted its forward motion—only a few feet away—though the harsh electrical noise grew steadily louder.

"That's what came down from the sky," Warren whispered to Roger. "Right after that red cloudburst. It looked like a black lightning bolt."

Roger nodded, his eyes fixed on the thing the in trees.

They had all tried to convince themselves they had not seen what they thought they had seen. That they had not actually passed through an unseen door to some unfathomable province from which there might be no escape.

That John Hanger had been nothing more than an unpleasant, ultimately forgettable stranger who had intruded briefly upon their pleasant evening.

Gradually, Warren became aware of a new, almost subliminal vibration—a strange sharpness in the air that made his scalp prickle—and he realized it was because another of the black lightning entities had materialized in the woods behind them, perhaps a hundred feet away, roiling and sizzling almost invisibly in the dark spaces amid the trees. There could be no mistaking the sentience of the things, the malevolence of them.

"We're being herded," Roger said, his voice barely audible. He pointed into the deep well of blackness beyond the nearest monster. "We're not supposed to go that way."

"Then we *need* to go that way," Kristin said. "Somehow."

Warren drew the engraved copper disk from his pocket and touched its cool surface. "I think the disks in the trees form a perimeter. When we solved that puzzle, it activated… something."

"You talk like it's something technological," Anne said, her eyes fixed on the black shape in the nearby darkness. "That's not manmade. It's *not* some technological marvel."

"How are we even seeing that thing?" Roger asked, staring at the nearest of the throbbing shapes. "It's just black inside of black."

"It's like the image is going past our eyes—straight into our brains," Anne said.

"My God, would you shut up?" Kristin whispered. "We don't know what they're going to do."

"They're not moving on us," Warren said. "Maybe we should just back away from here. The way we came. Slowly."

With no further words, they began to back toward the road, the snow gripping their feet with seemingly deliberate malice. Warren glanced back to make sure nothing else was approaching from the rear; he could see only uninterrupted black.

"They're not moving," Roger said. "Just blocking our passage. Like sentries."

"Then that's got to be the way out," Kristin said.

"It's just woods," Anne said. "Even if we got past them,

we'd never find our way through."

"Maybe over there, the woods just end. And we could end up back where we're supposed to be. That's why they're blocking us."

"I wouldn't bank on that," Roger said.

A few more steps, and they could no longer see the black things, though Warren could still feel, more than hear, a vague, electrical vibration in the air. "They're not following." But he looked with dismay at the pale stretch of snow and ice that extended before them into the dark woods. Would it lead only to another dead end? What was the purpose of all this—if there was one? Simply to freeze them to death?

Kristin kept looking back they way they had come. "I think we're making a mistake."

"Putting distance between us and them is no mistake," Roger said.

"How do you propose we get around them?" Warren asked.

"There are four of us," she said, giving him a grave look. "If we split up, maybe they can't catch us all."

"In the woods. In the snow. In the dark. With no idea which way to go. I don't think so, Crazy-Q," Roger said with a dismissive wave.

"And there could be more of them," Anne said. "No telling what's in those woods."

They plodded on in silence for a time until, as they rounded a long, sharp curve, they saw the very thing they expected and dreaded: another dead end.

"We're *have* to go into the woods," Kristin said, giving them all a long, thoughtful look. "Or we lie down here and wait to die."

Warren and Anne wrapped their arms around each other, trying to generate some warmth. In the last few minutes, the temperature seemed to have dropped even further. Roger heaved a sigh of resignation.

"I think she's right," he said at last.

Warren drew in a long breath, exhaled, and watched the steam jet from his mouth, swirl away, and vanish in the darkness. For the first time, both his heart and his mind were beginning to understand that there might be no escape from the unearthly trap they had sprung, save one.

He nodded. "Which way?"

"The way we're not supposed to go. Where else?"

Chapter Six
11:34 PM

Each of them turned on their phones, hoping against all reason that, somehow, their electronic devices might yet transcend this nightmare and find a signal.

Nothing.

Beyond the gray trunks of the nearest trees, the woods became a broken mosaic of black, white, and gray that dissolved into a featureless black gulf. Warren had always loved hiking in the woods, even in snow and darkness—but only when he was prepared. When the challenges he faced were the prosaic challenges of a world he thought he understood.

The wooded expanse ahead was a hellish dreamscape.

No sign of anything moving at the moment. No sound or vibration but for the wind whispering eerily in the distance. As they made their way between the trees, Warren kept his eyes open for any gleaming disks embedded in the trunks, not knowing why, but certain they were significant parts of this puzzle. After they had slogged maybe a hundred feet forward, he glimpsed something shining off to his right. He set off toward it, gripping Anne's hand and pulling her along with him. Sure enough, it was another disk, engraved with the strange characters, attached to a poplar in the same way as the others—as if it were as much a living part of the tree as the bark.

He remembered the toolkit he had slipped into his pocket, and he withdrew a flat-headed screwdriver, glancing at Anne so she could read his intentions.

"What do you think that will do?"

"No idea. Nothing, probably."

He placed the tip of the screwdriver at the edge of the disk and began working it back and forth, trying to dig deeply enough into the wood to pry the thing off. Even using all the strength he could manage, he couldn't force the tip beneath the disk's edge.

"Let me try," Roger said. "We'll get this bitch off here whatever it takes."

Warren nodded, handed him the screwdriver, and switched on his flashlight to illuminate the disk. Roger gouged and twisted, scraped away bark, shoved the handle of the screwdriver with all his strength, swearing with every breath. Finally, he whispered, "I think I'm getting it."

"Do we really want to do this?" Anne asked.

"Any reason not to?"

"Just hurry up," Kristin said, wrapping her arms around her body and shivering violently.

"I think I've—got it." There was a metallic *ting,* and the disk popped off into Roger's waiting hand. Warren aimed his flashlight beam at the tree where the disk had been attached. Apart from the screwdriver's gouging of the bark, there was no impression in the wood, no sign the disk had ever been affixed to the tree. Roger tossed the gleaming object to Warren.

"Looks just like the other," he said, turning it over. "Except there's nothing on the back. It's blank."

How the hell had it been attached?

"Look!" Kristin said, pointing into the woods. "That

wasn't there before."

Warren peered in the direction she was indicating. For a second, he saw nothing. Then he realized there was a tiny square of golden light burning in the distance, high above them. A window, he thought, and in spite of his deep sense that all was not as it appeared, his heart leaped. It *was* the first sign of human habitation since they'd left Stonewall.

"That's the way then," Roger said, giving Kristin a reassuring hug before starting forward. Anne shot Warren a thoughtful look, and he knew she felt the same reservations he did. Still, no matter what, they had to move on. They couldn't stay here.

"Keep your eyes open," he said. "That's still pretty far."

They had gone maybe a hundred yards, with at least as many to go, when the first electrical sounds erupted in the trees, somewhere to their left. He glimpsed a bluish flash, and his heart plummeted. Even if the yellow light represented some safe haven—and there was no guarantee it did—he knew they couldn't make it that far before the black things intercepted them. They were too fast, and the snow now seemed heavier, more impeding, than ever. His feet and ankles had already begun to scream with every step. Anne and Kristin surely had it even worse.

"Hurry," Kristin called, moving ahead of all of them, her eyes fixed only on the light at the top of the steep hill ahead. Roger put on a burst of speed as well, but almost immediately went down, ensnared by a hidden tangle of briers, sending up an explosion of snow as he fell. Warren heard fabric ripping as he tried to tear himself free of the spiky thorns.

"Motherfucking hell," Roger growled, reaching up to grab a low-hanging branch. Warren took hold of his other hand and hauled him upright. Kristin had not even slowed down.

To their left, the flame-like hissing and popping of the black lightning monsters grew louder, and Warren saw a flickering mass of brilliant black, fifty feet away, moving through the trees, not toward them but toward Kristin. He called after her, but she paid him no mind. Anne's voice joined in as the thing closed steadily on her. At last, her head whipped around, and she saw the thing, less than a dozen yards away.

Roger yelled at her, "Come back this way! Go to the right. To the right!" He took a few stumbling steps toward her but halted when he saw another black shape in the wake of the first, also moving toward her. "Come back this way!"

Anne pressed close to Warren. "That'll draw those things back toward us."

"We've got to stay together," he said. "If we get separated out here, it's the end." He took hold of her arm and began taking long, leaping steps toward Roger. Thankfully, Anne followed his lead.

Kristin began moving in a wide arc to the right but continued in the direction of the lighted window, rather than back toward them. She glanced back, and a blue-black flash highlighted her eyes; they were wide and blazing with panic.

"She's not going to make it," Anne whispered.

"Kristin!" Roger yelled, his voice now frantic. "Come back!"

She was beyond hearing them, Warren thought, for terror and adrenaline had overcome her. He could feel cold fingers of fear closing around the back of his own skull, and he began to call after her as well, certain it was all too late.

She was far enough away now that he could barely see her. And then, a moment later, she disappeared as the blackness fell upon her—a pulsating, living coil of pure energy, like a ball of onyx-hued lightning, closing around her body and swallowing her, simultaneously emitting a sharp crackling noise, which pierced Warren's eardrums like a serrated blade. The shock of it halted him in his tracks and sent him to his knees. With a pained hiss, Anne fell beside him and lifted her hands to cover her ears.

Kristin screamed: a long, raw cry that soared into the dark woods like a shrill dirge. Roger picked up a new burst of speed, rushing toward his wife as if the snow-choked branches, briers, and brambles were no more substantial than the frigid air. But the black, negative space that had closed over Kristin began to dwindle—speeding away from them as if returning with its prey to some dimension beyond the infinite expanse of woods.

"No!" Roger cried, his voice shrill with horror. "Kristin! No!"

His ringing cries rose into the otherwise silent night. The thing had taken Kristin and vanished, leaving the woods empty and still, yet no less menacing. Warren stood immobile, his muscles shocked into rigidity, his ragged breathing sending plumes of mist spiraling away into the darkness.

Somewhere, far away in the night, a faint scream rent the air.

"Kristin!" Roger called. "Kristin!"

The scream rang out again, this time even farther away.

"Oh, God," he whimpered, "No. No."

Warren felt Anne's fingers close around his wrist, and he drew her to her feet. Her hands automatically brushed the snow from her coat, and her eyes turned to the faintly glowing light of the window. Then she looked back toward the spot where Kristin had been taken.

"They're still out there," she said. "They're coming back."

He glanced at her. "What?"

"I can hear them. They're coming back."

He didn't hear anything, but he trusted her warning. Together, they slogged toward Roger, feet and fingers numb, their hearts hammering like fatigued pistons. He grasped Roger's shoulder. "We need to move. "

Roger shook his head vacantly, his eyes on the hidden boughs above their heads. Tears were streaming down his cheeks. "She's gone. I couldn't do anything."

Anne laid a comforting hand on his arm, then gripped it firmly. "We have to stay together," she said, her tone gentle. "We can't get separated. But we have to go."

"Go?" He barked humorlessly. "Where the fuck are we going to go?"

She pointed to the light beyond the trees. "That way. It's all we can do. Okay?"

He drew a long, deep breath and finally looked at her. He nodded. "Yeah. Okay."

They started forward, both holding onto Roger, who appeared ready to bolt into the woods at any second, his ears keen for any further sound that might indicate Kristin was alive. Warren found himself hoping they *wouldn't* hear her screams again; so piercing, even at a distance, and shrill with horror. Better to close his mind, block his emotions. If he relaxed his guard and allowed in the dread and grief that threatened to overcome him, he was as good as dead. They all were. He listened for any hint that the black things were returning, for Anne had seemed so positive. As yet, he couldn't hear anything.

Focus on the light. Only on the light.

When they had dislodged the disk from the tree, *something* had happened—something that had disrupted the alteration of space around them. If those objects did somehow generate a kind of barrier between the "normal" world and this one, it might be possible to break enough of them to escape. But was the lighted window a corner of their own world revealed, or just another manifestation of this one?

Clearly, Anne was wondering the same thing. Her pace faltered, and he realized she was staring at the light, now a hundred or so feet away. It was a rectangular window, to be sure, though they could see nothing on the other side—just a luminous, mottled haze, probably from closed drapes. "Do we really want to do this?" she asked.

"What choice do we have?"

She nodded, and they started moving again, though she twisted around to peer into the darkness behind them a couple of times. Barely restrained terror burned in her eyes.

"You still hear something?"

She shook her head. "Not right now. But that's almost worse."

"I heard something," Roger said, drawing to halt, his eyes flitting back and forth in the darkness. "Sounded like that noise—like before we wrecked."

Warren noticed it then too: a subtle but perceptible vibration in the air, as if something heavy had struck the earth some distance away. Then a deep, resonating *boom*.

"God, now what?"

"I think that thing in the sky *brought* the black lightning from somewhere else," Anne said. "And it's coming back."

"Maybe because we took out that disk," Roger said.

"Come on," Warren said, already starting toward the window again. "We keep going this way, and whatever happens…happens."

The other two were already on his heels, and now the heavy, rhythmic thunder blows were advancing, more rapidly than before. Warren could still see no sign of a structure at the top of the hill—just the glowing window amid a field of unbroken black. The embankment had grown steeper and choked with briers and brambles. The branches of the nearest trees were moving, and he thought the wind must have picked up, until he realized…no…the ground had actually begun to shake. A long strand of sharp briers, like a living tendril, wrapped itself around his leg, and he swore as he jerked free, offering some blood to the clinging plant. The heavy pounding was deafening, *consuming*, the individual sounds of impact becoming a continuous barrage of earth-shaking percussion. He thought he heard Anne calling to him.

In the sky, a gray, swirling haze was coalescing, its heart glowing warm red, growing quickly hotter, brighter. As before, Warren felt a hellish gaze beating down on him like the rays of a burning sun.

They were making no progress on the hill. Every step they took, the vines dragged them back and the deep snow shifted, keeping them off-balance.

He felt Anne tugging on his sleeve. She had to shout to make him hear. "It's trying to keep us from getting to the window!"

Downhill and to the right, he glimpsed a brilliant blue-black flash. The lightning monsters were on their way.

This was it.

"Look there," Anne cried, pointing to something a short distance to their right, between them and the oncoming black entities. The blood-colored shadows on the snow revealed a deep depression perpendicular to the incline and a dark opening where it met the hillside.

A culvert.

"Manmade," Anne said, leaning close to his ear. "What do you think?"

He nodded, grasping her point. He grabbed Roger's arm. The younger man still looked lost, barely aware of what was happening. "There. That may lead us out of here."

They made their way down the embankment toward the depression, and as they drew nearer, Warren saw that it was a ravine six to eight feet deep, the narrow stream within frozen solid. The mouth of the concrete culvert was a black void in the hillside, about four feet in diameter, its lower lip a couple of feet above the creek level.

Warren knelt in the snow at the edge of the ravine, switched on his flashlight—the light had grown disturbingly dim—and aimed the beam into the opening. The oblique angle allowed him to see only a short distance into the pipe, but it appeared free of obstruction, and he couldn't see any water inside, frozen or otherwise. He glanced up at the blazing red sphere in the midst of the cloud and then back to Anne. "If there's a way out of this…"

She nodded. Roger looked a little less distraught, perhaps galvanized by adrenaline. "Yeah," he said. "That's got to be it."

"How's your light?"

Roger switched it on. The beam was a tad brighter than Warren's, but his batteries wouldn't last much longer either.

The harsh hissing, popping noise of black flames alerted them to the rapid approach of the living darkness. Taking a deep, bracing breath, Warren forced himself to slip over the edge of the ravine. He came down in the midst of the creek, but the ice was solid and did not give way. Anne followed close behind him, and he grasped her arms to keep her from falling. Roger landed next to her, and then he turned around, automatically moving to help Kristin down after him. When he realized she was gone, his shoulders tensed, and for a moment, Warren thought he was going to break down.

"Come on," he said gently. "Let's just keep moving. All right?"

Tears glittered in Roger's eyes, but he nodded, clearly determined to remain stoic.

"I'll go in first and check it out," Warren said. "We don't

have much time."

Anne looked back down the ravine. "How do we know they can't follow us?"

He just shook his head, took a few steps toward the opening, and thrust his flashlight inside. The beam penetrated only twenty or thirty feet into the tube, but it revealed a smooth gray interior, free of debris or other obstruction, as far as he could see. It looked dry. Without hesitation, he stepped up to the lip of the pipe, grasped its upper edge with his free hand, and heaved himself inside. He had to crouch, but if the tube didn't get any narrower, at least they wouldn't need to crawl.

"It's okay," he called, his voice echoing eerily into the dark depths ahead.

With difficulty, he maneuvered around to face back the way he had come. The circular opening framed Anne's silhouette, and she hoisted herself up, coming dangerously close to cracking her head on the culvert's upper rim. He took her by the hand and pulled her inside. He could feel her body shivering violently. They crept in deeper to give Roger room to enter.

"All right, come on," he called. "Let's keep close together."

He heard a shuffling, scraping sound outside the opening and waited expectantly for several moments, but Roger did not appear.

"Roger, come on!"

His voice rang through the tube, but no movement came from outside. A cold stab of fear stopped his heart for a second. He and Anne remained crouched in their places, unable to make a sound. From somewhere out there, a burst of electrical crackling exploded through the ravine. He immediately switched the light off.

"God, no," Anne whispered, her voice cracking. "Please,

no. Please, no."

For countless long seconds, they heard nothing more, and, finally, Anne crept back toward the opening, Warren following close behind. She poked her head out and looked around at the night—now all too plainly empty, but for the glowing, eye-like sphere still gazing over the woods from above. She glanced down and exhaled sharply in fear and surprise.

"What is it?"

"Roger's flashlight," she whispered weakly. "It's lying out here."

Without warning, she slipped over the edge of the opening, and for a brief, horrifying moment, he thought she was gone as well. But she reappeared a second later, with the other flashlight in hand. "We may still need this." After pausing to regain her nerve, she hoisted herself back through the opening and grabbed his outstretched hand to pull herself into the tube.

"Do not do that," he said, trying to keep his voice steady. "You stay with me every second. You hear me? Every second."

She nodded, her eyes gleaming wetly in the reflected red light from outside. "I'm right behind you."

Crouching, he began to move forward, taking care to avoid striking his head on the concrete. He snapped the light on just long enough to get a clear look ahead: only an empty stretch of circular pipe that extended beyond the beam's range. When he switched it off again, he saw only endless blackness ahead. Behind him, beyond Anne's silhouette, he saw a dimly glowing circle that slowly receded as they moved forward, one shuffling step after another. His back wouldn't hold up to this crouching posture for very long, for he could feel a painful knot in his lower spine that constricted angrily with each step forward.

"You all right?" he called, his voice ringing at disconcerting volume through the confines of the tube.

"I'm okay."

They continued moving in silence for several minutes, until he lost all track of time and distance. He looked back again, and the opening had shrunk to a tiny, reddish pinpoint. Turning on the light again, he saw that the pipe stretched on endlessly. At least it was still dry and free of debris.

After continuing for some time longer, Anne called to him, "This is killing my back."

"Mine too. Let's rest a minute."

They settled into sitting positions, and Warren pulled her body close to his, rubbing her shoulders to generate some heat. The concrete felt frigid beneath them, even through their clothes and coats. But he had been cold for so long now he barely registered any discomfort. His hands and feet had gone numb hours ago, and the skin of his face felt taut and brittle. She pressed closer to him.

"I love you," she said. "I love you so much."

"I love you too."

He wanted to assure her that they were going to get out of this, but he knew if he said the words aloud, they would sound hollow and patronizing. He switched on his flashlight. The beam shone only dimly now, illuminating the passage a scant few feet ahead. "I guess I'm glad you grabbed the other light. Not that it's going to last long either." He switched his back off.

"I'm not liking the dark, I have to tell you."

"No. But it's a good thing it's freezing cold."

"Why?"

"If it were warm, there'd be snakes and rats and spiders in here."

"Thank you for that."

They went silent for a time, and Warren found his mind

shifting to Roger and Kristin. Was there any chance they were still alive? They had been such good friends. Oftentimes, Roger came across as crass and ill-tempered, yet at heart he was generous and loyal to a fault. And Kristin. He knew how deeply she loved Roger. Warren had found it difficult to accept her becoming a full-fledged psychiatrist, for he had always known her as a full-time student—youthful and occasionally irresponsible.

They could *not* be gone.

"How far do you think we've come?" Anne asked.

"Can't see the entrance anymore. A quarter mile. Half mile, maybe. I don't know."

"This is just an ordinary culvert. We *must* be heading back toward where we're supposed to be."

He nodded, then realized she couldn't see him. "Stands to reason."

"I guess we ought to keep moving."

"Yeah."

They hunched over and began shuffling forward again, the brief respite scarcely energizing. He hadn't gone a hundred feet before pain returned to blaze in his back and legs. Fatigue was starting to take its toll on him. Anne might be holding up a little better, but neither of them could keep going like this for much longer. He flicked on the light again, just long enough to see more darkness beyond the reach of its beam.

He heard it at the same time she did: a deep, echoing rattle from somewhere in the tube. Very faint—no way to tell which direction it came from. But it was clear that they were not alone in the enclosed darkness.

"Oh, God," Anne whispered. "The black lightning, I think."

The fire in his veins now drove him to move faster, and he heard Anne scrambling with renewed energy behind him.

Still, it was difficult to hold back a sudden, onrushing wave of hopelessness. If those things came after them in the pipe, there would be no escape.

"How far can this thing go?" she asked. "There's got to be a drain or a manhole somewhere."

A heavy thud echoed through the darkness, and Warren felt the vibration in his feet. He inadvertently straightened and struck his head on the concrete, sending a spike of pain through his skull. He was nearly spent. And for all he knew, they were hastening toward another dead end.

Then he saw it in the well of blackness ahead: a vague, misty glow: a spiral of light reflected on the walls of the pipe, still some distance away. The culvert must turn, he thought, and beyond the turn…some source of light. Not much to hope for, but enough to send a new surge of energy through his aching legs. He called back to Anne, "Do you see it?"

"Yes."

She had no sooner answered than another *boom* echoed through pipe. No way to tell how close its origin was, but it was far more powerful than before. When it came again, only seconds later, its sheer force nearly knocked him to his knees. He threw out his hands to brace himself, but Anne came up fast from behind and collided with him, sending him sprawling. He was back up in an instant and reaching for her hand. He could see her eyes in the reflected light, and they gleamed with pure terror.

Another heavy *boom-thud*. Deafening, jolting. *Unbearable.*

His legs moved automatically now. One hand was gripping Anne's and pulling her behind him. He didn't feel the impact when his head hit the concrete again. He just kept scrambling forward, a trapped rat, desperate to reach the illumination ahead. Then they were rounding the turn, and light washed over them, pale and murky, yet blinding after the pure darkness of the tube. It streamed down through a vertical tube, which rose to some inestimable height.

Otherwise, a dead end.

A series of metal rungs protruded from the cracked, ancient-looking concrete, leading upward. He grabbed the bottom-most rung and tugged on it. It held, but a few jagged shards of concrete crumbled from its mounts. He threw a glance at Anne. "It's the only way."

"Go."

"You first this time."

She looked back into the black tunnel from which they had emerged. Whatever was after them couldn't be far away now. "Just go. Go!"

He gripped the iron rung just above his head and pulled himself up, his right foot searching for purchase on the lowest. Then he was going up, hand over hand, his stomach lurching each time one of the ancient rungs shifted slightly. Anne followed closely, but after he had reached a height of perhaps twenty feet, she had fallen a little farther behind. She'd known she didn't have enough upper body strength to match his speed. Looking up, he saw a grille of iron bars that dripped wan, sickly moonlight, no longer blinding as his eyes grew accustomed to it. It was still a good thirty feet above him.

No choice but to keeping going up.

They had ascended about halfway up the shaft when Anne's voice drifted up to him. "It's coming."

"You can make it."

He looked down at her just as a new, terrific *boom* shook the tube, the shock sending flecks of dirt and debris raining from above. She was hanging onto a rung just below him when it pulled free of its mount, and he saw her flail frantically for a second, only to swiftly plunge into the murky darkness below. He heard a sickening crunch as she hit the bottom, and a shrill, agonized cry rang up through the tube.

"No! Anne!"

Her cries were piercing, her pain surely unendurable. He started back down, tears gushing from his eyes in torrents, and he realized a moment later that he was screaming too.

"My legs," she wailed. "Oh, God, I can't move."

"I'm coming back," he yelled. "I'm coming back."

"No! Don't you dare! Get out of here. Get out!" She began to sob horribly with each breath, but she continued to implore him, "Get out, please!"

Not a chance. He would not leave her down there, even if it meant certain death for both of them.

"I'm coming down!" Now he was whispering to himself, "I won't leave you. I won't leave you."

He hadn't gone far—he had just managed to maneuver past the missing rung—when she screamed again, this time in pure panic. Below, a thick, inky darkness, something between liquid and smoke, began to flood the tube, obscuring her from view, followed by the familiar, coarse, electrical crackling, loud enough now to drown her voice. Blue-black bursts of light sparked in the roiling storm below, and his arms and legs involuntarily froze—then, against his volition, began to carry him back upward.

"No, no," he groaned, somehow managing to stop himself. He was clinging to the rungs, still halfway between the hellstorm below and the vague light above.

The black lighting began to dance and writhe upward, striking at the lower ladder rungs like questing, greedy tendrils.

Then the bolts began arc toward him.

Anne was gone. He knew it. Like Roger and Kristin, all gone.

He glanced up at the wan yellow light, and for a brief

moment felt a pang of wistful longing. Then he let go of the rung and felt himself pitching into space.

Chapter Seven
Time Unknown

"Mr. Burr."

He shook himself, suddenly aware that he must have drifted off to sleep. The voice that penetrated the cramped darkness of his mind sounded deep but gentle. He didn't recognize it immediately, though it sounded familiar. Everything was black, and he could not remember where he was or what he had been doing.

A vague sense of unease began to throb somewhere in his consciousness. What was it? Had he been in accident?

"Mr. Burr," the voice said again. "Are you in distress?"

"No," he said, testing his vocal cords. His voice sounded many miles away. "I don't think so."

"Open your eyes."

He complied, or thought he did, for everything remained dark, at least at first. Then he realized a murky illumination surrounded him, and a brief jab of memory—something about Anne—brought with it a sharpening sense of alarm. In the misty blur before him, he could make out a dark figure some distance away. A very large figure.

Hang…

"John Hanger, you may call me," the figure said.

It all came rushing back.

"Anne," he groaned.

"I fear the young woman is no longer with us," John Hanger said. "Nor your other two friends. I am sorry."

He realized he was sitting in a hard, uncomfortable chair, his coat and gloves gone. The air felt cool and a little dank, and he smelled something musty, as if he were in a cellar. But as things began to take shape around him, he realized the room appeared more or less normal—dimly lit, filled with antique furnishings. A sitting room, he thought. Long, wine-colored draperies covered any windows. An ornate, Victorian lamp on a small table next to him provided the only illumination.

"You killed them."

"Indirectly, perhaps." John Hanger's mask-like face materialized in the shadows. It was smiling.

"Then I'm going to kill you." His voice sounded weak, impotent. So distant he hardly recognized it as his.

"That, I fear, is a declaration I have heard many times, over many years. More than you can imagine." He gave a little shrug. "Yet I am still here."

"Where is here?"

"Far from where you began."

A bolt of black lightning flashed in his memory. The sound of screaming. Anne screaming. He fought back a rising tide of grief. "Why?"

"A million questions, I am certain. Perhaps I will answer a few of them. I may ask a few of you, as well."

Warren realized he was slumped in the chair, and he tried to pull himself upright, but the expenditure of energy nearly sent him back into the darkness from which he had awakened. "Are you going to kill me too?"

Hanger was sitting in a large, throne-like chair in a corner, next to a set of long, flowing curtains, dressed in the same suit he had been wearing at Stonewall. His pallid face took on a pensive look. "I am not going to kill you, any more than I killed your friends."

"But you are responsible."

"That is what you believe?"

"Yes."

"Then you should believe that I am capable of much more than that."

Warren realized he cared little whether he died now or later. Anne was gone, and that was all that mattered. That, and the fact that John Hanger, sitting across the room from him, was her murderer. In the shadows, the big man's face looked like a grotesque construct of pale wax, the features crudely molded by palsied hands.

Hanger continued, "I confess I am moderately surprised that you are the one sitting before me. I might have expected it to be your young psychiatrist friend. Yet she was the first to lose her life. Isn't the unexpected challenging, Mr. Burr? I must say, I find it so."

Despite his aching desire to learn Hanger's purpose—his nature—Warren couldn't bring himself to speak and merely glared in fury and disbelief at the seated figure.

Hanger ignored him. "Of you, she was the youngest, certainly in best physical condition. Exceptionally well educated. An intuitive thinker. Yet her emotional reserves were apparently lacking, for she quickly became impulsive, reckless—even sooner than her husband."

"So you seriously misjudge people. Not very impressive."

Hanger refused to be riled. "That's not important. Thanks to you and your friends, my primary objective has been fulfilled."

"And what is that?"

Hanger leaned forward, his round, dark eyes bulging slightly. "What did you see, Mr. Burr? Tell me what you saw when things…changed."

Did Hanger honestly not know? He leaned forward as well, grasping the armrest to prevent himself slipping too far, and met the other's gaze. "Something in the sky. An eye, I think."

"Very good." Hanger did not elaborate further, his expression remaining neutral. "By the way, you deduced that you could effect certain changes by tampering with the medallions. They are called *Ahn Abzu Qip*, by the way. I congratulate you on your ingenuity."

"Too late for anything."

Hanger's gaze seemed to bore into his brain, and he reflexively averted his eyes. Not good, he thought. He felt as if he were coming out from anesthesia. As his senses grew clearer, more focused, his fear—his grief—began to rise again. Still, Hanger hadn't killed him immediately. He must yet want something from him.

Warren intended to deny him.

"How have you done these things? Why?"

Hanger's eyes had not so much as blinked. His voice took on a faraway tenor. "You have labored for an unimaginable time to alter circumstances you find unacceptable. It is a complex process that requires total dedication of mind, will, and body. Many trials. Tests. Once you determine your next course of action, you acquire what you need to proceed to that step. I have acquired you."

"Are you saying we're part of some experiment?"

Hanger's lips widened. "Very good, Mr. Burr."

"You did something to affect our minds."

"Perhaps, from a certain perspective. I assure you, however, that you have imagined or hallucinated nothing. All of your sensory input has been genuine."

Warren felt as disoriented as when he first realized the landscape had changed around him. For a moment, it had been almost a relief to believe that Hanger might have somehow drugged him and the others. Hanger's statement to the contrary struck him like a hammer blow, even though he knew—had known from the beginning—none of these incredible experiences had been drug-induced.

"What is it you want? Whatever you're doing, why bring us into it?"

"I require expendable subjects."

Hanger's eyes continued to glare at him, unblinking. He wasn't human. He *couldn't* be human. *What in God's name?*

He thought back to the frightened manager at Stonewall. "There have been others."

"Many."

Warren felt himself trying to shrink from the dark gaze, and he realized the back of his neck was sweating. Only now did the enormity of what they had faced tonight begin to dawn on him. At times in his past, he had idly wondered how it would feel to look on the face of God—or the devil. Surely, if this were not that moment, it was fast approaching.

He could no longer summon the words to speak to the figure before him. To his surprise, Hanger lifted something from a table next to him: a glass of red wine, which he tipped to his lips. His eyes swiveled back to Warren's.

"It is like a vintage I once enjoyed. In my original home, a very long time ago."

He replaced his glass on the table and leaned forward slightly.

"I know what you are wondering. Where did John Hanger come from? Who is John Hanger?" Warren felt sweat gathering at his armpits. "You are familiar with the Bible, Mr. Burr, yes?"

"Reasonably." His mouth was filled with sand.

"Think back to your Old Testament lessons. You may remember the story from your youth." Hanger's eyes finally left Warren's and focused on a spot somewhere on the far wall. "Once in Moab there reigned a King named Balak. A sovereign who cared for his kingdom and tended it as a gardener tends his prized garden. Also in those days, the Hebrews—the children of Jehovah—were expanding throughout the known world, conquering all the lands they believed their God had promised them." His eyes returned to Warren's, and his low, deep voice sharpened. "They showed little mercy to those who worshipped different gods than they. Balak foresaw his garden's doom, should these children gain a foothold upon it, so he endeavored to keep them out. And he did, for a time. He bargained with them. He enslaved some of them. He destroyed many of them. But there were sorcerers among them. Did you know this, Mr. Burr?"

"No."

"Oh, yes. Such truths have been excised or altered to make them more palatable to Jehovah's blind followers. These sorcerers were adept at placing curses upon the children of other gods, and they came into Moab, intending to dethrone King Balak. The king, however, brought one such sorcerer, who bore the name Balaam, to his side, and prevailed upon him to lay a curse on the Hebrews, that they might leave Moab forever. The sorcerer Balaam agreed. At the end, though, in act of treachery, the Balaam turned against Balak, and instead blessed the Hebrews, bringing about the king's downfall. 'Thus be to followers of false gods,' the children of Jehovah cried, and they moved unhindered into the garden of Moab."

The big man's voice lowered to little more than a whisper.

"But King Balak's gods were not false, Mr. Burr. Merely *other*. And seeing his plight, they bestowed upon him eternal life, so that he might from that time forth carry out their *will*, to pit himself against the God of the Hebrews, and all who might proclaim Him as their 'father.'"

Hanger's gaze burned into Warren's eyes like a torch flame.

"Do you know who I am?"

It was insane, yet all too plainly true. After all he had seen and experienced, he could not deny the evidence before him: that John Hanger was indeed the same King Balak of the Old Testament, somehow alive, somehow more than human. *Other* than human.

"Do you?"

Warren nodded. "Yes."

The great figure sat and glared at him in silence, and Warren soon felt as if ants were crawling over his body. The silence quickly became maddening, fearsome, and it seemed John Hanger—Balak—expected him to speak. Yet the idea of breaking the silence unbidden made his stomach churn with dread.

At last, the soft voice spoke again. "And now, Mr. Burr, we must proceed to the next stage. I doubt we will see each other again."

The finality of the statement set his heart racing, and he felt as if a slow blade were working its way into his chest. He somehow needed to break free of his fear-induced paralysis, get to Hanger, wrap his fingers around the giant neck, and throttle the life from this ancient, monstrous *thing* that had killed Anne—and Kristin and Roger. How to make his muscles obey his brain's commands? How to delay the monster long enough to make a move?

"Those symbols," he managed to croak. "Your medallions. How do they work? Why did you take control of our phones?"

The dark eyes looked thoughtfully at him. "All a means of

attuning you, physically, to the alterations of time and space. It's a simple matter to manipulate energy, to assume control of your electronic devices. Your interaction with them simply allowed me to access *your* information. Your data." He tapped his forehead to illustrate his meaning.

"What do you mean by 'attuned?'"

"To put it in terms you might understand, you passed between dimensions that exist on different wavelengths from the one you ordinarily occupy. Through your electronic instruments, I programmed you, so that you might become acclimated to the new vibrations without undue physical trauma. Others with whom I have experimented have been less fortunate. I could have achieved the same result using various alternative methods, but I prefer this one because it is *you* who initiate the process. Once the challenge is put in place, you inevitably strive to conquer it. Remember what the manager at the restaurant said? He called it a *game*. And so it is. At least that part of it."

Warren's heart sank further, though he might have suspected something of the kind from Hanger. "But what is your purpose—your goal—with all this?"

"Very well, Mr. Burr. I realize you are attempting to buy time. It will avail you nothing. But your curiosity is genuine, so I will tell you this: out there, in the far corners of the universe, in dimensions you cannot imagine, that is where the gods I revere exist. Upon the culmination of my experiments, under *their* guidance, I shall rend the barriers between the disparate planes of existence, which were never meant to converge. Then those other gods will rush in and remake creation in *their* image, bringing down all that that has been built by the minions of Jehovah. And for my part in their new advent, they will make me as they—eternal and incorruptible. Master of a kingdom unlike any that has ever existed. A new garden to tend on *my* terms."

Warren could not stop himself staring at the hellish thing on its throne. In spite of having witnessed so intimately this creature's sheer power, how could he believe these mad ravings? His mind went back to everything he could remember about physics, about religion, about *belief*. Finally, he said, "If your gods require *you* to do this, they must not be very powerful."

"All gods use intermediaries, even yours—which, if you had any concept of its true nature, would send you fleeing in terror. Jehovah is merely a name devised by humans for the primal force they cannot begin to understand. Now. We are arguably fortunate enough to exist on a plane of time and space that intersects with many others. From this plane, there are terminal points that I have learned to access. Witness the shifting of dimensions you experienced tonight, the unleashing of those entities that reside on the other side. At the farthest, chaotic ends of reality, where the other gods exist, these barriers are far more numerous, and much more difficult. Make no mistake; eventually, perhaps eons from now, they would surely break through on their own. But now their return is imminent, and *I* am the facilitator."

Warren felt himself sweating again. *He is simply a madman; a monstrous, murderous lunatic who has somehow gotten inside my brain. His name is John Hanger, not Balak. Just John Hanger.*

"And now I must leave you. If you survive the transition that is to come, I will know the time is right; that I myself will be able to pass through the barriers into spaces that even I have never seen. If you do not survive…then my work is not yet finished. I will have to start again on this phase. But I am above all things patient, for I have seen the passing of many years."

Hanger rose from his seat, downed the last of his wine,

and offered Warren a curt bow. The bastard was going to get away. But Warren could still scarcely move. His limbs felt sluggish and heavy, as if a great weight were pressing down on them. Even if he could catch up to Hanger, what could he do? He lacked the physical strength to overpower the big man.

He saw a dark, arched portal at the far end of the room. It had not been there before; he was certain of it. Without a look back, Hanger passed through it, and Warren was left alone.

Chapter Eight
BEYOND TIME

The silence in the chamber overwhelmed him. A total absence of sound and vibration, as if even the atoms of the air had ceased their movement. He realized he couldn't hear his heartbeat or his breathing. He placed a hand on his chest; he could feel a steady beating beneath his ribcage, and only when he concentrated could he detect the faintest rhythmic thudding in his ears. He exhaled deeply, and a low, muted hiss told him that he hadn't gone deaf—not completely, anyway.

He could move again. As soon as John Hanger had exited, the weight that pinioned him to his chair seemed to evaporate, and most of his strength quickly returned. He rose to his feet, tested his weight, and took a few cautious steps toward the tall chair Hanger had vacated. The chamber's lighting appeared dimmer now, the shadows in the corners deeper and more ominous. He made his way to the nearest set of long draperies and pulled them aside, only to reveal a blank, ivory-toned wall. The portal through which Hanger had passed was the sole visible exit. He was reluctant to follow the big man into the dark passage beyond, but he could hardly remain where he was. Even if Hanger's foretelling of some nebulous "transition" were the ravings of a lunatic, no help would ever find him here—wherever *here* was.

Ahead, he saw a long, shadowed passage, almost as dark as the culvert he and Anne had negotiated. A few steps into it, a gust of frigid air rushed over and overwhelmed him, as if the shadows themselves were drawing the heat from the atmosphere, from his body. He glanced back—and then froze, for it was happening again: the portal to Balak's chamber had vanished, leaving him in an empty, virtually lightless corridor that extended into wells of darkness in both directions. But *some* illumination remained, he realized, for he found himself standing in a pool of dim, copper-hued light. He saw, just above his head, a dully glowing spot in the ceiling—one of Hanger's medallions, just beyond his reach. For a second, he recalled how *something* had changed when Roger had detached the disk from the tree in the woods, and he wondered if he might yet somehow thwart Hanger's plan. But even if he could reach the disk, with his coat gone, he no longer possessed any kind of tool to dislodge it.

The weight of defeat fell upon him again, but now his feet automatically carried him on. Something in the passage was changing: the *character* of the darkness, the density of the shadows. Streaks of color swam within them—blue and violet, even a few hints of blood red. He could discern no other source of illumination; just a strange, intermittent shifting amid the lightless space.

And the silence was no longer complete.

A deep, almost subliminal *thumping* sound. Slow, rhythmic. He recalled the sounds they had first heard after they had left Stonewall. This was similar, maybe identical.

Hanger—Balak—truly *was* mad, yet he had somehow manipulated the very foundations of reality. And he intended to topple them.

Warren stopped in his tracks, only now fully comprehending the personal significance of Hanger's plan.

If he survived the "transition," it meant Hanger could survive it.

If he survived, it meant the end of everything.

He no longer doubted a word Hanger had told him. But what if that ancient, undead monarch's work had not progressed as far as he had anticipated? How long would it take for him to complete his work anew? Weeks? A year? A century?

Only with his own death could Warren defeat Hanger and avenge his friends. He had to pray for a fatal flaw in Hanger's design.

Personally fatal.

He could see an island of pale, golden light ahead, swimming amid a bizarre mosaic of blue and violet shadows. Looking down, he felt a moment of vertigo, for a huge mass of cloud appeared to billow far beneath his feet, as if the floor had become transparent—or dissolved, though he remained standing on a solid surface. And he could still hear the rhythmic thudding sound, which he perceived as somehow infinitely distant, yet near enough to shake his body down to his bones. He took another tentative step forward, but his foot came down on something *else*. No longer a solid floor, but something that yielded beneath his weight, almost immaterial—as if his body had been become magnetized, and he had stepped onto an identically charged space, its force repelling him, preventing him from toppling into the yawning abyss that had opened before him.

My God.

The corridor had vanished, and he was now standing *within* the vast space, facing a cluster of stars—some kind of galactic cloud—laced with all the colors of the spectrum, surrounded by an endless expanse of pure *blackness*. His head began to swim and he felt his body lurch, overwhelmed by the sense of having been swallowed by space itself. The distant pounding drove deeper and deeper into his skull, into his very spirit, drawing nearer with every beat. He now detected something else accompanying it: an erratic, flutelike chirping—faint, almost subliminal—but profoundly disturbing, maddening, as if it were a voice, unintelligible but unmistakably directed at *him*.

Beyond the immense galactic cloud, he detected motion. A subtle tendril of color—violet blue, maybe—extending, *twisting* into view, dragging behind it a swirling mass of cloud, which grew steadily brighter as it slowly revealed itself to him.

In the center of the cloud, a monstrous, golden-red eye opened, its gaze blazing across that immeasurable gulf to fall directly on him. Now a new, consuming dread rushed in, displacing the fear he had known in John Hanger's presence. This, truly, was one of Balak's *other* gods—something spaceless and timeless, something that existed on a plane *beyond* existence. The image of this thing that he and Anne and the Levermans had seen—it had been a reflection, a ghost; a mere insinuation of the horror that lay somewhere beyond any known universe.

It was for *this* that Balak intended to tear down the barriers of reality.

Of sanity.

Warren felt a terrible heat building inside him as that infinitely distant gaze lingered on him. And yet he welcomed it, for surely, this meant his death was imminent. And if he died, Balak was thwarted. At least it bought time.

He would rejoin Anne, and that was all that mattered.

Hotter and hotter inside. He realized his feet were no longer planted on any surface. He was floating in a sea of black flame, of *negative* flame, and for a second he thought he heard a vague, distant hissing sound.

The black lightning. The minions of Balak's alien god.

The inner fire was becoming agonizing. He *was* going to die.

Thanks be to all that's holy, for there must still be something *holy in this universe.*

All became black.

Black.

Chapter Nine
6:24 PM

"Warren?"

He shook himself, wondering what had come over him. He felt lightheaded and nauseated, but he had no recollection of what had brought it on. Anne was staring at him with a little smile on her face.

"Sometimes, I swear, you are a dizzy old man, do you know that?"

"What?"

"Deaf, too."

He looked around and discovered he was standing in his living room. The lamp in front of the window glowed, creating a comfortable pool of golden light in the shadowed room. Anne had just put on her heavy coat.

"Roger and Kristin will be here in a minute."

His thoughts—*everything*—still seemed jumbled in his brain, and he realized he felt relieved to be here with her. He knew it was early evening; the curtains were still open and, outside, darkness had fallen. He went to the window and peered out, comforted by the familiarity of his own home, yet disconcerted to have lost some unknown measure of time.

What the hell?

Outside, it was *very* dark. He couldn't even see the snow that covered the front yard. Something about that was not right.

"Warren, are you okay?"

He turned to look at Anne.

She was supposed to be dead.

No, no, she was not dead, she *couldn't* be dead. What in God's name was he thinking?

God's name.

Gods.

Other.

Gods.

He was alive.

He had survived.

"Oh. Oh, no."

"Warren?"

He looked at her, saw concern in her eyes. From somewhere outside, far in the distance, he heard a deep, heavy boom. She heard it too and leaned forward to peer out the window.

Anne was here, alive. But she *had* died. He remembered now. She had fallen.

Time had shifted.

The foundations of the universe were toppling.

From outside, a golden red light began to spread across Anne's face.

Something in the sky was opening its eye.

END

About the Author

Stephen Mark Rainey is author of the novels *Balak*, *The Lebo Coven*, *Dark Shadows: Dreams of the Dark* (with Elizabeth Massie), *The Nightmare Frontier*, *Blue Devil Island*, and many others; over 200 published works of short fiction; six short-fiction collections; and a trio of audio dramas for Big Finish Productions based on the *Dark Shadows* TV series, featuring several original cast members. For ten years, he edited the award-winning *Deathrealm* magazine and has edited anthologies for Chaosium, Arkham House, Delirium Books, and Shortwave Publishing. Mark lives in Greensboro, NC. He is an avid geocacher, which oftentimes puts him in some pretty scary settings. Visit his website at **www.stephenmarkrainey.com**.

Other Books by Stephen Mark Rainey

The Last Trumpet
Balak
Dark Shadows: Dreams of the Dark (with Elizabeth Massie)
The Lebo Coven
Blue Devil Island
Other Gods
The Nightmare Frontier
The Gaki & Other Hungry Spirits
Legends of the Night
Song of Cthulhu
Evermore (with James Robert Smith)
Deathrealms
Fugue Devil: Resurgence
Deathrealm: Spirits